CW00517894

Basics of Business M

Booklet 3

Marketing Management

(Customer is the king/queen)

A.S. Srinivasan

Clever Fox
PUBLISHING

Chennai • Bangalore

CLEVER FOX PUBLISHING
Chennai, India

Published by CLEVER FOX PUBLISHING 2023
Copyright © A.S.Srinivasan 2023

All Rights Reserved.
ISBN: 978-93-56482-17-3

This book has been published with all reasonable efforts taken to make the material error-free after the consent of the author. No part of this book shall be used, reproduced in any manner whatsoever without written permission from the author, except in the case of brief quotations embodied in critical articles and reviews.

The Author of this book is solely responsible and liable for its content including but not limited to the views, representations, descriptions, statements, information, opinions and references ["Content"]. The Content of this book shall not constitute or be construed or deemed to reflect the opinion or expression of the Publisher or Editor. Neither the Publisher nor Editor endorse or approve the Content of this book or guarantee the reliability, accuracy or completeness of the Content published herein and do not make any representations or warranties of any kind, express or implied, including but not limited to the implied warranties of merchantability, fitness for a particular purpose. The Publisher and Editor shall not be liable whatsoever for any errors, omissions, whether such errors or omissions result from negligence, accident, or any other cause or claims for loss or damages of any kind, including without limitation, indirect or consequential loss or damage arising out of use, inability to use, or about the reliability, accuracy or sufficiency of the information contained in this book.

Marketing Management

*Based on my booklet **A Concise Guide to Basics of Business Management**, I thought it would be appropriate to outline major concepts and practices under each functional area as well as business strategy in greater detail in the form of booklets. Thus, along with the **Concise Guide**, these booklets will give a more detailed coverage of these concepts in the field of business management.*

Of course, each concept in itself has been covered and discussed in great detail by many scholars and there are innumerable books on each of them. No one small booklet like this one, can claim to do justice to all of them in a few pages. This is just a distilled and brief outline of them which again is intended to give an overview of these classic concepts so that the reader becomes familiar with them.

*I have reproduced my Introduction, References and Afterword from my booklet **A Concise Guide to Basics of Business Management** since these booklets will also serve the same purpose to the same audience and are from the same sources. Nothing stated here are original and are based entirely on the materials mentioned in Introduction. I was fortunate to have had the opportunity to study them. Where necessary, I have taken the liberty of using them to preserve their meaning. The errors and misunderstandings are purely result of my limited knowledge and exposure.*

***Booklet 3** in this series is on **Marketing Management**. Major topics in Marketing Management like Customer Orientation, Segmentation, Targeting and Positioning, Managing the Marketing Mix, Marketing Strategy are covered here. Marketing invariably attracts the interest of a newcomer to the field of management, and I hope this booklet leads to further enquiry into topics of interest to you.*

A.S. Srinivasan   **October, 2022**

A Concise Guide to Basics of Business Management

Introduction

This booklet will be of use to all those who are interested in the field of Business Management. If you are a practising manager or an entrepreneur, this could serve as a refresher. If you have recently taken up a managerial position, this will be a useful reference book for you to look at some of the concepts mentioned here. If you are a student or a person interested to know the basics of management, this will serve the purpose of a guidebook.

This booklet is brief but comprehensive, outlining all the major management concepts and practices in all functional areas. As a manager in today's highly competitive and dynamic business environment, you need to

1. *Develop the capability to look at your organisation's business holistically*

2. *Become familiar with major concepts and practices in all functional areas of management*

3. *Understand the integrated nature of your business, the interconnectedness of various functions and the impact of your individual and departmental decisions and actions on the total operations of the company and*

4. *Have the urge to develop yourself further to meet the challenges of today and tomorrow*

Hopefully, this booklet will help you embark on this journey of life-long learning.

I have primarily relied on various management books by leading authors in compiling all the concepts presented here which I gratefully acknowledge. I claim no originality or ownership of these ideas. I have gathered these over the years I was serving in academics. I have appended a list of primary references and have mentioned the names of original thinkers and writers in my text at appropriate places. There are many more that are in public domain which I have used in presenting these contents.

All these classic concepts have been mentioned very briefly and need further study for greater understanding. This is in no way a textbook. It is just a window to the field of management. This booklet will have served its purpose if it arouses your curiosity to know more on any topic or concept you are interested in. I look forward to receiving your comments and feedback.

Welcome to a short journey through this fascinating field of management!

A.S. Srinivasan   **October, 2022**

Marketing Management

As we go through this Booklet 3 on "Marketing Management", it will become evident that marketing is an activity in which each member of the organisation is involved directly or indirectly in serving the customer and collectively, their participation has profound impact on its marketing success.

This booklet will cover the following major topics in the field of Marketing:

1. Understanding customers and markets

2. Segmentation, targeting and positioning

3. Managing the elements of marketing mix

4. Managing customer relations, managing brands and integrating marketing communication

5. Developing marketing strategies

6. Taking marketing "beyond marketing"

1.   The marketing concept:

1.1   "Business is Marketing":

Marketing people are fond of saying that "business is marketing" since business involves finding a customer need and fulfilling it at a profit, which is the objective of marketing too. Marketing is primarily an exchange process where the organisation and the customer exchange goods and services for a surplus or profit over costs incurred for the organisation and adding value to the customer.

1.2 "Marketing" definitions:

There are several formal definitions of marketing all conveying similar meaning. A comprehensive definition given by the UK Chartered Institute of Marketing is as follows: "Marketing is the management process responsible for matching resources with opportunities at a profit by identifying, anticipating, influencing and satisfying customer demand".

1.3 Three elements of marketing process:

We can say that there are three elements involved in the marketing process.

- Customer: Fulfilling customer need is the basic objective of marketing and the marketing process starts with the customer and ends with the customer. In his seminal article titled "Marketing Myopia" in 1960, Prof. Theodore Levitt of Harvard Business School made a strong case for customer orientation as follows: "Companies should stop defining themselves by what they produced and instead reorient themselves towards customer need". An automobile company should not consider itself as a car manufacturer but consider itself to be in the business of providing transportation to the customer. This automatically widens its scope of activities by reorienting its focus on customer need.

- Organisation: Organisation has the necessary resources and turns out products and services that match with customer demands.

- The marketing environment: Companies do not operate in vacuum. They operate in an environment consisting of customers whose needs they are aiming to satisfy, competitors who are also working to satisfy same customer needs, government with its policies and regulations and of course, the larger society whose needs too are to be met. Further, this environment undergoes constant change due to evolving technologies and resultant innovations, changing customer demographics, tastes and perceptions, governmental regulations, once again leading to greater competition.

From these, we can see that marketing involves continuous understanding of customer needs and wants through dialogue, translating these to other departments in the company and coordinating their efforts towards fulfilling customer needs and maintaining customer relationships.

1.4 Development of marketing concept:

The development of marketing concept as the primary driving force in business went through some distinctive phases. Though marketing or selling as a part of commerce and trade existed since a long time, it is only from about mid 1920s that importance of marketing/selling was felt. Until then, since demand was always ahead of production, the emphasis was on improvement of production efficiency. The classic example is the development of mass production of interchangeable parts and assembling them on moving assembly lines in the automobile industry by the great manufacturing genius Mr. Henry Ford. He famously stated: "I will give the customer any colour as long as it is black", indicating the primacy of production efficiency in those times and total disregard for customer choice.

However, when industries became more competitive, the emphasis shifted to "selling". Here, the aim was to convince the customer "somehow" with aggressive selling techniques that company's offerings were the best that money could buy.

Only much later starting in 1970s that the importance of customer choice became the driving force in business. This is the birth of the so-called modern marketing era. Since then, with advent of new manufacturing, information and communication technologies, customer supremacy was firmly established. Practices like relationship marketing, societal marketing, online marketing, involving the customers in co-creation, social media marketing etc have all become standard practices. The basic idea is to put the customer first in the whole chain of business.

Notwithstanding these developments, many companies continue to operate under hidden emphasis on profit maximization and production efficiency, often leading to their decline and demise.

1.5 Delivering customer value:

As we saw, an organisation can fulfil its purpose of making profits and creating wealth to the owners only by fulfilling a customer need or want and retaining the customers by offering them a value higher than what competition or others offer. This is the basic premise on which all businesses operate to remain viable.

1.6 Perfect markets and market breakdown:

As per economic theory, perfect markets are charecterised by several sellers and buyers, all with full knowledge and information about the product and there are no constraints of availability of requirements to produce the product to all producers/sellers and there are no constraints of choice to customers.

However, in real life there are no perfect markets and markets break down due to imperfect competition, asymmetric and incomplete information etc. In fact, marketers create and thrive on these imperfections or distortions to their advantage.

1.7   Marketing regulations:

Hence, we need market regulations primarily for the following reasons:

i.   It is a fact of business that healthy competition is a must for protecting the interests of all stakeholders in the way business is conducted. This is to ensure that customers have a choice to fulfil their needs, suppliers get their due payments and the government and public at large get due taxes, environmental protection etc.

ii.   There are no true monopolies except in the case of certain public goods and services often run by government. Near monopolies (where there is just one large supplier), duopolies (where there are two large suppliers who dominate the market) and cartels (a group of suppliers controlling supplies and prices)- all these are detrimental to the interests of customers. It is the duty of government to minimise this risk and encourage healthy competition in industry through regulations.

iii.   A corollary of this is that you need regulations to protect the interests of the customer or buyer. Without marketing regulations, sellers will often tend to make false claims to lure the customers to their products and services. "Caveat Emptor" is a common legal phrase which ultimately put the onus on the buyers advising them to be on guard since it is their responsibility to make sure that what they buy meets with their requirements. In real business world, sellers protect themselves from possible defects through offering warranties/guarantees to compensate the buyers for defective product or poor performance. Regulations are necessary to protect consumers' interests in such instances.

iv.   Finally, we need marketing regulations to ensure that the consumers get the right quality and right quantity of product as declared by the supplier. For example, there is Packaged Commodities Act that requires the manufacturer to declare quality standards, contents of the product and Maximum Recommended Price (MRP) etc on the packages and other legal provisions to ensure this.

1.8   Ethics and social responsibility in marketing:

Apart from governmental regulations, companies and marketers have developed their own codes to ensure that their actions are ethical and socially responsible. While these are guidelines, actual behaviour and actions depend on the values of the individual companies and their marketing staff. Some of the guidelines cover:

*   Ethics and products: Do companies have policies covering new products and new markets? For example, some companies in India do not enter business of liquor products. Some companies in the USA do not enter new markets which they consider violating human rights.

*   Ethics and promotion: Do company's advertising and sales promotions conform to generally accepted standards and society's ethics and values?

*   Ethics and selling: Do company's marketing people oversell the product advantages and give wrong sales pitch to potential customers?

2. The marketing environment:

2.1 The marketing environment:

As we had seen in booklet 2 on Organisations, we can define the marketing environment as consisting of three circles:

- Your organisation's internal environment which you can control.

- Near environment consisting of customers, competitors, suppliers etc which you can influence.

- Far environment dictated by wider sociological, technological, economic and environmental factors (STEEP factors) to which you can only respond.

We list below the various factors in each of them which need to be studied and understood.

i.   Sociological: Demographic profiles like age, sex, education, occupation, urban and rural, gender roles etc, structure of families like nuclear, joint, extended etc, religious and cultural traditions and practices, consumption and shopping priorities, patterns etc.

ii.   Technological: General current technological practices and emerging trends, impact of new technologies and industries, resultant job obsolescence and emerging new skill requirements

iii.   Economic: When we look at the larger economic scenario in the country, some of the major factors to be considered are:

- Rate of economic growth: How is the economy growing, measured by GDP? Which sectors, which markets?

- Inflation rate: This will indicate the movement in prices to see whether they are in line with growth.

- Interest rates: Related to inflation, you can find out what the real returns are.

- Rate of unemployment

- Exchange rate of national currency

- Cost of industry inputs like power etc

- State of infrastructure

Taken together, they represent the state of the economy.

iv. Environmental: Pollution levels, Level of deforestation, changes in climatic conditions etc.

v. Political:

- Stability status of central and state governments
- Policies and legislations on general areas like health, safety, reservations etc
- Taxation and trade policies on property, income, sales, customs etc
- Corporate governance policies and laws like statutory reports on income, ownership etc, auditing requirements, Corporate Social Responsibility (CSR) etc
- Trade blocks and trade agreements etc

2.2 Competitor analysis:

In the near environment, as marketers our concentration will be on customers and competitors. We will first look at analysing competition.

Studying and understanding competition is essential because it is dynamic and keeps changing with changes in the wider business environment. It affects all aspects of our organisational activities. We need to be on our guard all the time, anticipate competitive developments and respond both proactively and reactively.

We need to study the strengths and weaknesses of all major competitors in following areas:

- Organisational
- Management
- Marketing
- Strategic actions and the company's position in the industry

We do this based on our experience in the industry, published industry data available in public domain and through networking with our contacts. As marketing persons, we are uniquely placed to undertake this analysis and can act as the eyes and ears of the company.

2.3   Environmental analysis:

Normally, companies go through several stages in scanning and analysing the external environment. Starting with a wide, undirected, overall scanning of all that is happening in the external environment, they go down to more directed viewing and informal and formal research. To get the most out of environmental scanning, companies should look out for any relevant information, however far removed it may be from their present operations. They should also constantly broaden their sources.

As we had seen in booklet 2 on Organisations, it is the ability to pick up and make sense of "weak" signals that distinguishes a leader from the pack. While strong signals are seen by everybody in the industry, the leader will be better prepared to make use of unknown and developing opportunities by locating the weak signals from the din and noise in the environment.

2.4 Forecasting:

Based on their observation and analysis, companies use several forecasting techniques to predict future course of events. Some of the major forecasting techniques are:

- Extrapolation: Using statistical tools, companies extrapolate past and present trends into future. Some of the statistical tools used include time series analysis, correlation and regression analysis etc. But in today's dynamic environment, these have limitations.

- Marketing research: Several marketing research techniques are used which we will see later.

- Judgment: Here, views of selected experts in the industry and business environment form the basis for forecasts.

- Models: These are advanced and sophisticated mathematical and statistical models that are developed for specific requirements.

- Scenarios: Under scenario planning, company assembles its managers and teams are formed to write what future will look like. These are not based on statistical models, but the teams present future scenarios like stories based on what they think are relevant, important but uncertain future developments. These help the companies prepare robust strategies to meet any eventual future event. Often quoted example of scenario planning is scenarios developed by Shell Oil Company which helped the company in meeting the challenges of oil crisis in 1970s.

A word of caution here is that it is always advisable to use multiple forecasts rather than a single point forecast since you can never forecast future accurately.

It is the job of top management and marketing persons to do environmental scanning constantly to keep abreast of latest developments.

2.5 Developing competitive advantage:

As we had seen in Booklet 2 on Organisations, an organisation delivers value to all its stakeholders using certain resources at its disposal and putting them all together to create and deliver value. The main resources a company can bring in are:

- Financial: Cash resources, accessibility to financial markets like banks and other financial institutions, Private lenders (sources of debt) and stock markets (equity) etc.

- Physical: It invests part of these financial resources into plant & equipment, technology, R & D etc.

- Legal: It can hold patents, copyrights, licences, trademarks etc.

- Human: People resources combine all the other resources to deliver value. They consist of number of employees, their knowledge, skills, commitment etc.

- Organisational: This includes the structural strengths, cultural characteristics etc.

- Relational: An organisation's relationships and networks with its customers, shareholders, employees, creditors, suppliers etc serve as a major resource.

15

- Informational: In modern data driven business world, knowledge about business environment, customer preferences and emerging trends, competition etc is a great resource.

Resources by themselves do not produce results. But a combination of resources brought together in an optimal mix for the tasks on hand, produces the results expected. This is called capability. Thus, while resources form the basis of firm's capabilities, capabilities alone give it competitive advantage.

In a competitive situation, as a general rule, we can say that there are two requirements for a firm to succeed. First, it should have some specific advantage over competitors. Secondly, the company's products should be the preferred one in the "buy" basket of customers, at a price which covers the costs and margins of the company. The firm can achieve these by analysing competition on one hand and customers and markets on the other.

This analysis should lead the firm to arrive at how to gain advantage over competitors and also what factors influence customers' choice. Thus, the factors required to succeed in a competitive industry called the key success factors, are derived from this twin analysis of customers and competition. We had earlier seen the factors to be considered in analysing the strengths and weaknesses of competitors in our industry. We will now move on to steps we need to take to understand our customers and markets. Marketing persons are in regular touch with the customers and their first point of contact with the organisation. Hence, they are uniquely placed to understand the customers and their needs and translate them to the rest of the organisation. Thus, the role of marketers as the link between customers and the organisation cannot be overstated.

3. Some basic points for common understanding:

Before we move on to the section on Understanding customers, we will look at some basic points so that we have a common understanding of the words used.

3.1 "Market":

The word "market" can mean any of the following:

- A place where buyers and sellers meet and where exchange of goods takes place. It could also be used to denote the type of product or service sold like vegetables market, real estate market, commodities market, stock market etc.

- As a measure of total demand for a product in a particular region/country/world in money or quantity terms like total market for petroleum products in tonnes, diamond market in terms Rupees, toilet soap market in terms of units and value etc.

- Trade is another term used to denote the industry dealing in a particular product, like oil trade or construction materials trade etc.

3.2 B2B and B2C markets:

In a market situation, there is generally a buyer and a seller. Buyers can be individual customers, organisations, government etc. Similarly, sellers can be individuals, companies etc. We use the terms customer and consumer interchangeably to denote buyer, though there is a subtle difference. Thus, we talk of

- B2C markets where the seller is a business organisation and the buyer or consumer is an individual. Invariably, the products sold are called consumer products or fast-moving consumer goods (FMCG).

- B2B markets where both the buyer and seller are organisations and the products are called industrial products.

Their characteristics differ as we will see later.

3.3 "The offering":

A company may be offering a product which normally denotes the physical aspect or it may be offering a service which is often invisible. However, in reality there are no pure products without a service element or services that do not have a product content. Hence, we call products and services as "offerings". We will be seeing more of this under elements of marketing mix.

3.4 Market potential:

We need to consider the following factors when we try to establish the total market size or potential demand for our offering:

- People who have a need for our offering. Very often, new products fail because companies are not able to find sufficient number of people who need them.

- We should consider their purchasing power. Though there may be people with an unmet need for our offering, they should have sufficient purchasing power.

- We also need to understand their buying behaviour- what factors motivate and influence them to buy etc.

4. Understanding the customer:

We will now embark on our journey towards developing our marketing strategies the first step in which is understanding the customer.

4.1 Customer decision making process:

The rational customer decision making process can be seen as consisting of following steps:

- Need recognition: There may be an existing or a latent customer need. Customers may also be made to "want" a product or service even when there may not be a "need" through marketing messages by companies.

- Information search: The customer then starts looking at information on which products and brands will satisfy his/her need/want.

- Information evaluation: This information is then evaluated by the customer using his/her own criteria for selection.

- Decision: At this stage, the customer makes the buying decision.

- Post purchase evaluation: The customer evaluates the actual performance based on his/her criteria and takes suitable decision on whether to go for repeat purchase or not.

Following are the limitations of this classical approach:

- Customers need not/will not go through all steps for all products. In fact, in low-cost items, many times it is a question of availability and impulse buying at the point of purchase.

- They need not follow this order. They may even make the decision first and then work backwards to justify the decision.

- Often, decisions will not be taken on rational consider-ations alone. Even in purchase of major items, other emotional and psychological factors come into play and decisions reversed at the last minute.

4.2 Influences on decision making process:

This leads us to analyse the influences on the decision-making process of the customer. They could be:

- Individual's (the buyer's) own influences
- Group
- Supplier or seller
- Situational

4.3 Individual (customer's personal) influences:

It goes without saying that in any decision-making process, ultimately the individual's influence or thinking leads to the final decision. This is based on psychological factors like perceptions, attitudes and motivation.

Perception is the process by which an individual organises and interprets information received from various sources to create a meaningful picture of what comes in as input. Thus, it is not just a passive process, but shaped by individual's interpretation. Ultimately, for the individual perception is reality.

Attitude towards a subject is a position taken by an individual that leads to the person's disposition or reaction to it, like positive or negative.

Motivation is a bunch of forces that drive us to do certain things or behave in certain ways. They could be both internally and externally generated.

We will see later in this booklet, how companies try to "manipulate" or "influence" a person's perception, attitude and motivation through advertising, sales promotion and other communication.

4.4 Other influences:

These include:

- Group influences by which the person, driven by a sense of belonging, conforms to his/her group's decision.

- Supplier or seller influences: As we will see later, companies try to influence the customer's decision-making process through clever and strategic planning of their marketing mix elements.

- Situation influences: These often influence the decision-making process by the situations created by markets, weather conditions and other external forces beyond customers' control. In a time of shortage situation, they buy up things to last longer.

4.5 General factors that influence customers:

Apart from the above, following general factors influence an individual's buying behaviour:

- Age, sex, education, occupation, social class, geography, religion, cultural background etc which are covered under the demographic characteristics.

- Income levels, lifestyle, peer pressure etc. These are in addition to personal characteristics covered under psychographic factors.

- General economic conditions which may lead to greater or lower income levels, availability etc.

4.6 The purchase process:

This follows customer's decision-making process and the various stages are known by the acronym AIUAPR. These are self-explanatory as given below:

A - Awareness: The customer becomes aware of the product or service being made available.

I - Interest: The customer gets interested and wants to know more about it.

U - Understanding: He/she develops an understanding of what it offers in terms of features and benefits.

A – Attitude: A positive or negative attitude develops and positive attitude leads to buying.

P - Purchase or the act of buying.

R – repeat; If satisfied, the customer goes for repeat purchases.

Both internal and external factors come in to play, which we will discuss later.

Like any rational model, this too has limitations.

- Customer need not go through all stages.
- He/she need not follow this sequence of stages.
- Many purchases are made more on impulse and/or emotion rather than following this rational process.

However, the model helps the marketers understand the customer buying process and plan how they can influence them at each stage through suitable interventions and communication.

5. Understanding business markets for industrial products:

5.1 B2B markets:

There are some basic differences between business or B2B markets and consumer or B2C markets as given below:

- Generally, there are a few large buyers in B2B markets.
- There is direct and close relationship between customer and supplier.
- Since these products have certain technical inputs and specifications, often the purchase decision is taken by professional technical people.
- Normally, there are only a few middlemen like dealers etc and it is direct purchase by the buyer from the seller.
- In many instances, B2B markets are concentrated in certain geographic areas due to concentration of buyers industries there.
- The demand is often derived from demand for the final product of the buyer.
- Demand for B2B products is often more fluctuating than consumer products due to changing economic conditions and fluctuations in markets for buyers' products.

5.2 Understanding B2B buying process:

Unlike consumer markets where the purchasing decision is taken by a single consumer, there are several players in the industrial product buying process. They consist of:

- Initiators, who start the purchasing process.
- Gatekeepers, who keep the flow of information between various members involved in the process.
- Influencers, who provide the technical and other inputs for buying decision.
- Controllers, who decide the budget.
- Deciders, who make the final decision.
- Buyers, who place the orders, follow up on supplies, effect payments and complete the buying process.

In small companies, only a few people are involved in the buying process but in large organisations, you will find the entire team of participants listed above.

5.3   Stages in B2B buying process:

Just like the general, rational problem-solving process, there are several steps in industrial products buying:

- Recognition of the need or problem
- Deciding on quality specifications and quantities required
- Looking out for and finalising potential suppliers
- Getting proposals giving price quotations, terms of sales and analysing and comparing them
- Selecting the most suitable supplier
- Negotiating and finalising prices and other terms and conditions of supply
- After receipt and use, evaluating the supplier and giving feedback for course corrections on regular basis and also rating suppliers, if there are more than one.

We can see that in industrial product buying, more rational decision making is involved, more people are involved and more negotiations take place. This also offers considerable scope for developing personal contacts, personal selling opportunities and relationship building with customers while in FMCG products, we rely more on our brands and advertising and other sales promotional strategies to do these functions.

6.   Marketing research:

We will now move on to a major strategic tool in the arsenal of marketer's toolkit, marketing or market research. While it may just be semantic, they say that marketing research includes researching on all aspects of marketing whereas market research is confined to study of consumer and market behaviour only. We will use both terms interchangeably here.

In today's information world, accessing reliable information, picking up the "weak" signals as we saw earlier, making sense of them, getting the necessary insight ahead of competition- these give great competitive advantage to the company. It is only through marketing research that companies can gain this customer insight. Marketing research is a vast science and today with the advent of many advanced scientific models, companies are able to gather massive and precise data, analyse and make sense of them. This section can hardly do any justice to this major field.

6.1   Fundamental purposes of market research (MR):

Basically, marketing research is carried out to meet the following objectives:

* Reduce uncertainty in decision making while developing marketing strategies since this may affect the business strategy of the organisation. It helps in making informed decisions but it should be kept in mind that no forecast/projection based on market research can be 100% accurate.

* Help in monitoring performance. Once decisions have been implemented, continuous monitoring research helps in finding whether the company is on track to achieve its objectives and how far it is fulfilling the expectations of the customer.

* Keep track of developments in the environment which is vital in the strategic process. MR helps in finding out

changes that are taking place in terms of new and developing technologies and changing customer profiles and preferences.

Thus, marketing research findings form the inputs to company's decision-making process especially in matters relating to overall strategy, marketing decisions etc.

6.2 Major marketing research methodologies:

Apart from own sales force and other sources like trade channel partners, normally companies employ outside agencies for MR since this is a specialised field and also to avoid bias in carrying out research. Various methods by which marketing information is gathered can be grouped into primary and secondary research.

6.3 Secondary marketing research:

This involves collecting information from relevant published materials and records. They could be internal like company's past records or external, available through industrial bodies, government and private enterprises. Companies also buy reports published by individual agencies for a fee and also participate in a syndicated research where many players in the industry participate for general macro data.

6.4 Primary research:

This is based on information collected by doing direct surveys /research in the market. They could be qualitative or quantitative research.

i. As the name implies, qualitative research is carried out primarily to find out qualitative information on product quality, consumer perceptions, testing new product ideas etc. Normally, these are gathered by conducting focus group studies, in-depth interviews with a few experts or users and also through detailed observation. These are done by experts who are able to initiate and facilitate discussions in an unbiased manner and summarise the findings in focussed group interactions. In-depth interviews and observations help in picking up certain qualitative insights which may not come out in group discussions.

ii.   Quantitative data is collected through carrying out larger surveys and experiments. These are used to arrive at quantitative information like the total size of the market, market share of different players including our own, factors considered by customers including non-buyers while choosing a product with rankings, brand awareness, brand image etc. Some of the important factors to be considered while embarking on quantitative research are:

- Defining the objectives of the exercise and briefing the market research agency clearly on these

- Questionnaire design involving what questions to ask which are relevant to the objectives. Also, it should be kept in mind that too long a questionnaire that requires a long time to complete should be avoided. Care should be taken to see whether the questions are close-ended or open-ended, depending on the purpose of that question.

- Sample size: The number of people to be contacted and surveyed depends on the objectives, estimate of total population, confidence levels to be achieved, budget allotted for the exercise etc.

- Sample selection: Several statistical techniques are used to decide on what kind of people should be surveyed. It could be based on random sampling, stratified sampling, focussed sampling etc.

- Administering the survey: The most important criterion here is that biases should be avoided while conducting the survey. This calls for trained persons and strict supervision, back-checking etc. The way the surveyor presents himself/herself and conducts the survey are critical factors in the quality of information collected. As said earlier, companies normally entrust marketing survey assignments to reputed MR agencies known for integrity and competence. Of course, cost will be a factor to be considered.

- Collection, tabulation, calculation and interpretation of data- all require special attention. Certain sophisticated statistical techniques may be required calling for the services of specialists.

- In many instances, record keeping becomes important so that these surveys can be repeated with the same respondents if we are trying to measure before and after a particular marketing action's impact.

6.5   Uses of marketing research and avoiding pitfalls:

Very often, biased assumptions or hypotheses lead to defective design, implementation and interpretation of results leading to wrong conclusions and thereby wrong decisions. At strategic level, this may lead to wrong strategic decisions threatening the very existence of the company. One of the most often quoted examples is the story of New Coke which was introduced by Coca Cola in 1985 to match/better the main rival Pepsi Cola, after blind taste surveys, only to incur heavy losses and re-introduce Coca Cola Classic.

Information and conclusions based on well-researched data will help strategically in

- Changing the basis of competition to company's favour
- Strengthening customer relations
- Generating new products

6.6 Positioning, perception and preference:

We will now discuss one of the major applications of marketing research, finding out consumer perceptions and preferences.

Normally, companies develop a positioning platform as a major input to their total marketing strategy. Positioning is how the company wants the customers to see its product and what position the product should occupy in the minds of the customer. On the other hand, perception is how customers actually perceive the company's product and what position it occupies in their minds.

Through suitable marketing research methodologies, we try to find out consumers' perception about our product with respect to competition on chosen attributes. Taking it one step further, consumers' perception and preference may also differ. As an example, we can say that people saw "Nano" as an economy car, which was the position the company presumably wanted to establish. However, many customers did not prefer or desire an economy car since they were looking at other attributes as well.

6.7 Perceptual mapping:

There are two methods which are used to find consumers' perceptions of several competing brands on multiple dimensions or attributes, as given below:

- Attribute rating method
- Overall similarity of pairs of products/brands method

  i. Attribute rating method: Here, we can choose the attributes in which we want to rate all major competing brands and, in each attribute, we can rank the brands in performance in that attribute from the lowest to the highest as perceived by the customers. Similar ratings can be plotted for all attributes. This will give a picture of how your brand and competing brands are perceived by customers and how they are ranked in their minds.

  For example, if you decide that "freshness" is an important attribute in a toilet soap, you can rate and plot all competing brands including yours, between "giving maximum freshness to minimum freshness" so that you can see how consumers perceive your brand with respect to competition in "freshness".

  ii. Overall similarity method: Here, a pair of important attributes are chosen which form the axes in a 2x2 matrix. Brands with similar consumer perceptions are grouped and located in the four quadrants which gives an idea what brands are perceived similar to yours. This is used where we cannot verbalise the attribute very well in the way the customer would understand. Odour, taste, aesthetics etc are some such attributes.

6.8 Conjoint analysis:

i. Conjoint analysis is a comprehensive but a complicated marketing research tool. It is used to estimate an individual's "value system"- how much value a customer puts on each level of each attribute of the product/service.

We know that a product has a number of features and attributes relevant to the customers. In the conjoint research exercise, the consumers react to a number of alternative levels of each attribute and the value they attach to them. From this, we can measure each attribute's importance and the most desired level of this attribute to the consumers. They are offered several trade-offs – increasing the level of one attribute by reducing the level of another attribute and so on to arrive at the preferred level of each attribute and optimal bundle desired by the customer. Before carrying out conjoint survey, we have to find out through another survey what individual attributes consumers look in for, relevant to our product category.

ii. One example of a company that had used conjoint analysis with other marketing research tools is Marriot group of hotels in the USA. When they found that the market for their full-range, high-end chain of hotels, located in busy areas, was nearing saturation levels, they carried out extensive market research to come out with a new hotel concept. The result was the Courtyard by Marriot chain of hotels which was aimed at business and middle level security-conscious travellers whose needs were not served in the industry. They built in features and attributes that matched with their requirements. These travellers placed more emphasis on security, bed and bath comfort and a built-in office table and were willing to settle down for self-check-in, limited range restaurants and not city-central locations for a given price. Ginger group of hotels from Tata's is also based on similar approach.

iii. The bottom line is that if companies carry out marketing research scientifically, they are bound to get the much-needed customer insight that will help in formulating successful marketing strategies. However, very often

31

research projects end up being biased and not well-planned with the result that they lead to disastrous results.

7.   Segmentation, targeting and positioning:

We will now move on to one of the most important pillars of marketing strategy, in fact, of business strategy itself. If we get our segmentation, targeting and positioning right, half the battle is won.

7.1   Segmentation:

A basic marketing axiom is that "you cannot be everything to everybody". This is where segmentation comes in. it Is the process of grouping customers and potential customers within a market into different groups or segments, consisting of customers having the same or similar requirements which can be fulfilled by a suitable and appropriate marketing mix strategy.

Attacking the entire market is like shooting with a "shot gun" with no specific target whereby the misses are much more than hits. Segmentation is similar to aiming and shooting with a pistol where the chances of each shot being successful are great. This way your success rate will be high and you can conquer the entire target market successfully, making the most of your marketing spend.

7.2   Segmenting consumers:

Consumers are grouped into segments based on the following variable factors like demographic, geographic, psychographic and behavioural.

- Demographic: Age, sex, race, religion, education, income, occupation, family size, family's life cycle (what age groups in the family)
- Geographic: Urban, rural, city size, state size, climate, nationality
- Psychographic: Lifestyle, personality, social class
- Behavioural: Benefits desired, purchase frequency, usage occasion, brand loyalty, attitude towards brands, price sensitivity

7.3 Segmenting B2B markets:

Similarly, B2B markets can also be grouped into segments based on following factors:

- Benefits desired from product: Product performance, durability, economy, ease of usage
- Benefits expected from supplier: Delivery time, service reputation, ease of doing business
- Organisational factors: Location, size (Sales, number of employees etc), industry group, financial position, reputation and years in business
- Behavioural factors: Frequency of purchase, quantity of purchase, purchasing approach, price sensitivity, type of purchase (new, repeat)

7.4 Segment characteristics:

We need to find out the following characteristics of segments before we can assess their attractiveness to our business:

- Size: Total size of the segment
- Identity: Can the segment be identified and targeted as a group?

- Relevance: Is it relevant to our offering and how relevant is our offering to the segment?

- Accessibility: How easy/difficult it is to reach the identified segment in terms of supplies and promotions

7.5 Attractiveness of a segment:

Based on the above, we should be able to assess whether the segment is attractive for us to focus on, based on the following:

- Size of the segment and its growth potential

- Profitability of the segment in terms of returns we can expect by serving the segment

- Current and potential competition in terms of their relative strengths and weaknesses

- Capabilities of our organisation: Do we have the capabilities to meet the expectations and meet the demand of this segment?

7.6 Targeting approaches:

Having decided on the segment/s, we have several targeting approaches as under:

i. Undifferentiated: Here, firms can target the entire target market or all segments. Normally, this targeting approach is chosen when

- It is a young and growing market where there is not much difference between customer requirements in various segments including price and performance

- Firm's brand image is high

- Firms have the option of adding on some features for a specific segment, retaining the overall basket of features

ii. **Differentiated:** Here, firms can choose to target either a few segments with differentiated offerings or focus on a few segments with one offering:

- **Customised:** This is where firms tailor-make their offering to suit the needs of one particular customer

- **Niche marketing:** This is the concept where you target sub-segments within a segment by making your offering suitable for their requirements. Many small companies may opt for this since they can make optimum use of their limited marketing resources.

7.7 Mass markets:

Even in undifferentiated targeting approach, large companies develop different positioning and marketing mix strategies for the same product to appeal to different segments. An example of this is the approach of soft drink giants like Coca Cola and Pepsi who straddle all segments of the mass market with suitable positioning/promotional strategy for different segments for the same product.

7.8 Positioning:

i. With segmentation and targeting in place, positioning strategy is possibly the most crucial aspect in a company's overall marketing strategy. If you get your positioning right and succeed in occupying the appropriate position in the customer's mind as the most preferred brand in the category, i.e., if your target consumers' perception matches with your positioning, your marketing mix strategy has done its job.

ii. As we had seen in the earlier section on Marketing Research, positioning is how the company wants the consumers to see its products /services and what position they should occupy in the minds of the consumers.

iii. We had seen in Booklet 1 on Introduction to Business and Management that an organisation can fulfil its purpose of making profits and creating wealth to the owners only by satisfying a customer need or want and retaining them by offering them a value higher than what competitors offer. I reproduce below what we have already seen in Booklet 1 since positioning strategy is primarily the marketer's responsibility. We had further defined customer value through an equation as

Customer value = Benefits – costs

iv. We also know that the product or service is offered as a bundle of values to the customers superior to that offered by competition so that it occupies the pole position in their minds. Benefits offered to customers consist of the following:

- The product or service offered that meets with their requirements in terms of price, performance, functions, features, technical innovation, product/service assurance through creating and managing brands etc.

- Availability and reliability of supplies on time and in quantities required.

- And overall experience with the product and company in terms of services, solutions and other intangible factors like brand associations etc.

- The costs incurred by the customer include price paid, other acquisition costs like transport, maintenance etc, payment terms in terms of credit facilities, discounts offered and ease of getting the product.

36

v. Organisations can prosper only when they are able to create or discover value, deliver part of value to customers and retain balance as can see be seen below:

- Customer value = Product + Access + experience

- Value discovery consists of developing a product or service that provides a value which is greater than that offered by the next best competitor in that class.

- Value delivered which is also called as consumer surplus, is the additional value offered to the customers over the nearest alternative, from the value discovered as above.

- Value retained or captured which is also called as producer surplus, is the balance of value discovered less value delivered to the target customer. We can express this by the following equations:

- Value retained or captured = Value discovered or created – Value delivered to customers

vi. Further as explained in Booklet 2 on Organisations, in today's highly competitive markets, companies who are innovative, resort to special positioning strategies as given below:

- With the development of highly sophisticated marketing research tools and techniques like conjoint analysis etc, companies are in a position to understand the preferences of customers in various segments more accurately. Based on these insights, companies are able to develop and offer new product concepts and positioning strategies which are altogether different from existing products and services in an already over-crowded market/industry. This concept of strategic space positioning in uncharted waters, developed by Profs. W. Chan Kim and Renee Mauborgne is aptly called the "blue ocean strategy" as against red ocean where existing companies fiercely compete with each other with marginally differentiated offerings.

- This they can do by developing "value curves" for each segment. Value curves represent what features and benefits the customers in that particular segment would be willing to pay for and what they would be willing to give up instead. Thus, for each segment, you can incur more "good costs" to incorporate these preferred features and benefits and reduce or eliminate "bad costs" on those that customers would give up. You can also arrive at what customers would pay for this offering. We had seen examples of Courtyard by Marriot hotels chains in the USA and Ginger chain of hotels from Tata's in India.

- Another special positioning strategy is called "reverse positioning" and allied new positioning strategies. Here, the companies are able to create new strategic space by moving away from established segments and creating a new segment/segments.

- An example of this is the positioning of IKEA, the European furniture manufacturer. They succeeded in the American furniture market by borrowing features of the extreme ends of the market. One is the high-end, multi design, full range, high inventory, expensive chain furniture shops offering advice from specialists on furniture selection. The other end consists of minimum quality, minimum range, minimum cost, low-end single shops. IKEA created a new segment of cost-conscious segment of young customers, making shopping experience as the main attraction. The company offered minimum range in each type of furniture, standard quality acceptable at the price offered, self-assembly and self-transportable furniture in completely knocked-down condition in flat packages. Thus, they eliminated all "bad costs" for this segment and added on "good costs" to be incurred to give that unique shopping experience. By sourcing components from all over the world at the lowest costs, the company's total costs were brought down. Thus, they created a new value curve.

- Similarly, Starbucks made coffee drinking extremely popular in the USA where it was not a major market. At one end, there were high speciality single stores offering exotic flavours of coffee at very high prices. And there were many small, lowly-differentiated, low-cost stores at the other end, offering minimal coffee experience. Starbucks came in with two distinct value propositions- one, a big range of speciality coffees to suit well-to-do individual customer's tastes and two, personalised attention to individual customers. Their chain of coffee shops in multiple locations were tastefully decorated providing private space for customers. They were seen as "a third place, apart from home and office". Thus, coffee drinking in Starbucks was seen as a personal indulgence, since they charged the highest prices, a new position for a new segment.

- Through gaining insight into preferences of hitherto unknown and unserved market segments, these companies created an altogether new strategic positions and dominated the markets as leaders.

vii. Experiential marketing: Companies execute their positioning strategy through a mix of various elements which is called the marketing mix consists of 4 Ps of marketing – Product, Price, Place, Promotion. We will be discussing these in detail in the following section.

However, companies need to ensure that perception of consumers regarding their offering matches with that of their positioning promise. They do this today by moving from focussing purely on features and benefits to focussing on enriching consumers' experience with the offering, consisting of sensory, emotional and intellectual experiences. This is called experiential marketing. Each experience with the offering from getting to know about it till consuming it, should reinforce this position/perception match.

8. Managing the marketing mix:

Of all marketing concepts, the most commonly used by marketing professionals is the concept of marketing mix. The term "marketing mix" coined by Profs. Jerome McCarthy and Neil Borden of Harvard Business School, has been in use from 1950s. As stated by the much-celebrated marketing guru Prof. Philip Kotler in his textbook on Marketing in 2000, it can be defined as "the set of marketing tools that the firm uses to pursue its marketing objectives in the target market", thus lending itself to be called as a broad mix of various marketing tools.

All the tools are grouped into "4Ps" of marketing – Product, Price, Place and Promotion. Subsequently with increasing share of services, three more Ps were added – People, Process and Physical Evidence. One major criticism of the 4Ps approach was that it was highly product and producer oriented. Later on, they developed "4Cs" and "4As" to make it more customer-oriented and communication-oriented, all conveying the same elements as follows:

4Ps	4Cs	4As
Product	Customer needs & wants	Acceptability
Price	Cost	Affordability
Place	Convenience	Availability
Promotion	Communication	Awareness

We will now see each of these elements in greater detail.

9. Product:

9.1 Defining products and services:

Products include the physical product, its features, specifications, packaging etc. But we can say that in real life, there are very few products which are only physical, may be like rice, salt etc. On the other extreme, companies produce or offer very few services which are purely intangible like consultancy, travel etc. Hence there is often a mix of both product and service in what a company offers to its customers. We will call this as "offering", a product-service mix. Almost all products have a service element in them and similarly, almost all services have a product element in them.

9.2 Characteristics of services:

However, there are some characteristics which distinguish pure services. They are:

- Intangibility: Consumers cannot see, touch, feel or experience a service before buying it. Hence word-of-mouth recommendation or a recommendation from a user to a non-user is important.

- Inseparability: Services are produced, sold and consumed at the same time and hence cannot be produced and stored in inventory for a sale later. Customers are also a part of this process. The quality of service cannot be checked before it is delivered. This indicates that the front-line staff who deliver the service are critical in creating a favourable experience and hence the importance of professional training for them.

- Heterogeneity: Unlike products, there is a lot of human interaction between the customer and the person delivering the service and hence differences, in the process of service delivery. This again reinforces the importance of selection of right persons, training and motivating them.

- Perishability: Since services cannot be stored, meeting the seasonal fluctuations in demand is a challenge. Will the company over-staff or under-staff, will it create over-capacity or work with under-capacity?

All these factors make marketing of services more challenging.

9.3 Experiential marketing:

With growth of Information technology and standardisation of mass-manufacturing processes, products have become "commodities" with very little difference between competing products in the market. Hence, companies resorted to adding on more of service element in their offering to give greater value to the customer and gain competitive advantage. However, over a period of time the bundle of services too gets copied nullifying any advantage. As we had seen earlier, companies now try to offer a different experience through experiential marketing elements so that it becomes very difficult for competitors to replicate and offer the same kind of experience to the customers.

9.4 Types of products:

In a very broad sense, we can classify products into following categories:

- Innovative: These products are totally new to the market.
- Adaptive: Here the existing products are modified to suit changing customer tastes.
- Imitative: These products are based on a strategy of copying or improvising on what is already available in the market. Invariably, small companies which enter a competitive market for the first time adopt this strategy of "follow the leader".

It is a fact that almost 95% of new product launches fail. This could be due to several reasons including and primarily misunderstanding the consumer preferences and trends.

Also, while being the first mover offers several advantages, it is also a double-edged weapon. If consumer acceptance is low, the first mover may not have the sustaining power to last through the introductory stage. Here, there is a risk of a more resourceful and agile operator taking over the leadership and reducing the innovator to an "also ran" player.

Depending on imitative products is also risky since the innovator and the immediate followers would have built enough features in the product that it will be difficult to imitate them completely.

9.5 Product Life Cycle:

We will now take a brief look at another concept in marketing, "Product Life Cycle (PLC)". This is best represented by a bell-shaped curve as the product goes through successive stages of:

- Introduction
- Growth
- Maturity
- Decline

These are self-explanatory. Marketing strategies required at each stage of product life cycle are different. However, the overall, total life of a product and at each stage vary with the nature of the product, customer perceptions and later on acceptance, gaining mass support either in selected target markets or undifferentiated markets and competitive forces etc. Decisions on changing strategies would be done after thorough research and acting before the inflection point at each stage.

In today's dynamic business environment with convergence of new technologies resulting in new products and new applications, product life cycles have become shorter. Hence there is a great need for companies to continuously innovate and keep developing and introducing new products, though as we saw earlier the success rate of new products remains low. This leads us to the topic of New Product Development.

9.6 New Product Development:

i.   An integral part of marketing mix is "New Product Development (NPD)". We saw just now that every product undergoes a life cycle. As it grows and reaches maturity level, profits from the product starts declining. Any further expenditure incurred on additional marketing promotions and other activities will not earn sufficient margins to offset the extra costs and profits from the product starts falling down. However, as we know, companies can grow only by increasing sales and profits year on year and whole business world is driven by the objective of growth in profits.

Hence it is imperative that companies have several new products in various stages of development in the pipeline so that they can introduce one after another as the previous profit leaders mature and profits start declining. They should also have a strategy of planned product obsolescence so that new, improved products that fulfil customers' expectations better, can be introduced.

ii. We should also know that new product development is a lengthy process consisting of several stages like:

- Researching/innovating a new product idea called concept generation
- Testing the concept and developing prototypes
- Retesting and modifying the prototype
- Planning for and getting ready for manufacture to meet expected initial demand
- Finalising marketing strategy
- Introducing the new product in the market
- Nurturing it and putting it into growth phase

At each stage, it is essential that the company keeps its eyes and ears open to get customer feedback for improvements as well as competitive developments, while monitoring general business environment on a continuing basis. In spite of this, as we had seen earlier, 95% of new products fail due to several missteps and misreading of the market or wrong assumptions and conclusions. We know that how a product concept like Nano car failed.

iii. As this booklet is taking shape, we are in the midst of the most unprecedented emergency in our lifetime. It is over 5 months since COVID-19 virus has struck humanity and the best of pharmaceutical companies are yet to come out with a viable vaccine that could prevent further devasta-

45

tion at the earliest. No doubt, the whole development process from concept generation to final manufacture and distribution is very lengthy and has a lot of strict guidelines for testing etc to be followed. Yet, many of the vaccines being developed may not be successful. It is the same case with any new product development process, though these are abnormal times and the challenges are too great.

Subsequently, as I am editing the booklet during end September, 2022, a good number of vaccines have been developed with varying degrees of effectiveness and a lot of human misery has been avoided in the last one year. But an equal number of new vaccine development efforts have also failed.

9.7 Analysing the "product":

i.   To help us gain insight into the concept behind any product, we can look at it in three levels:

- Core product: This is the basic benefit offered by the product to the customer. For example, in the case of a car, the basic benefit offered is moving from one place to another or transportation.

- Actual product: This is sum total of the physical product that has certain features, attributes and benefits. In a car, it is the physical appearance of the car, the engine and seats are the features and speed and comfort are the benefits.

- Augmented product: In a car, this includes all the benefits loaded on like radial tyres, safety belts, airbags, self-locking windows etc, etc.

Companies keep loading their products with a lot of additional benefits which they consider as offering value to the consumers. They may incur additional costs but offer greater value to the consumers. Here, we can recall our earlier discussion on value curves, adding "good" costs and eliminating "bad" costs to arrive at new offerings to selected target audience who value them. The basic concept to be remembered here is that features are what companies provide in their offerings, but what consumers see/seek in them are the benefits that will accrue to them.

9.8 Differentiation and branding:

i.   We have just seen that the core product is the basic benefit that the product offers to the customers. Thus, products from all companies that offer the same benefit are the same product. This is the nature of commodities. However, the marketers try and invent new core benefits to the customers by adding on some additives or features to make their product stand apart or differentiate it with respect to competition. This is called differentiation with the basic purpose of giving the product a unique identity. This is also called as the unique selling proposition (USP) of the product.

From the customers' point of view, we can say that the core product includes the need satisfied by the added features. These could be stated, unstated or latent wants or needs. As an example, we can say that while cleaning teeth is the basic benefit offered by all toothpastes, companies add on additives to offer whiteness, elimination of bad breath etc as additional benefits and make them the USP of their toothpastes, thus converting a commodity into a product.

ii. However, with availability of real time information today, all competitors catch up with company's innovations in a very short time. Thus, product differentiation loses its competitive advantage. Hence companies started adding on more and more service elements to attract and retain their customers. This too has its limitations since all these also get copied by all competitors in no time.

iii.   Further, to make the customers perceive their product as different and superior, armed with data from marketing research, companies added on physical, rational and emotional or psychological differences through several measures like positioning through advertising and other sales promotions, special packaging, after-sales benefits etc. Thus, the product with this bundle of features, attributes and benefits, becomes a brand and branding gives the company's product a unique image and personality. The progression from a commodity to a product to a brand is complete. We will now move on to see briefly how brands have become an integral part of our day-to-day living.

9.9 Brands:

i.   A brand represents several aspects of the company's offering to the customer. At one level, it stands for the product or service offered by the company. At a physical/tangible level, it is a name, trademark, proprietary sign, symbol or a logo. At a psychological and emotional level, it represents a concept, a promise or a benefit. Figuratively, we may say that while the company may "create" the brand, it is the customer who gives his/her own meaning to it or "owns" the brand. Thus, a brand may mean different things to different persons.

ii.   Functions of branding: Based on the above, we can say that following are the functions of branding:

- Obviously, it differentiates your offering from those of competitors.

- It stands for ownership- who owns/promotes the brand.

- It is used to communicate your offering's capabilities.

- As we saw earlier, brand allows consumers to express their preferences.

- It works as a risk reducer for the consumer since he/she can expect same standards of quality/price/performance, as desired.

- Companies use brands as a strategic intent- it represents what strategy is followed by the company to differentiate its offering.

- Thus, it is a comprehensive expression of all the company's product/service offerings as well as how consumer perceives them. It is the sum total of company's positioning of its offering and customer's perception of the same. As we said earlier, when positioning and perception coincide, it becomes a successful brand.

iii. Successful brands: Elaborating on this, we can say that through their brand, companies offer a bundle of functional and intangible benefits which are consistent with one another and give the offering a unified, unique identity and character.

From the customer's point of view, successful brands combine physical, rational and emotional appeal into a distinctive blend of clear identity. Customers see and accept these brands as offering them the best value in the category. Thus, brand is not just a name, but a bundle of benefits. We will see how companies manage their brands later in detail.

10. Price/cost to the customer:

It is generally said that if you get your pricing right, you have won the battle. Even with all modern research techniques, pricing is still an art to be mastered by all in the company since it directly affects the company's profits in more ways than one.

10.1 Calculating the price:

There are three major elements that are to be considered while you fix your selling price or cost to the customer.

• The first element is estimating the total costs that go into making the product and reaching it to the customer.

• You then have to check what competitors' prices are for a similar product or a product that offers same bundle of benefits to the customer.

• Finally, and most importantly, you have to find out what expectations your present and potential customers have, from your product at the price they are paying. This is an area where even experienced marketers fail.

10.2 Pricing systems:

Correspondingly, there are primarily three pricing systems:

• Cost-related pricing: Here, the company first estimates the total costs involved in making and delivering the product to the customer. It then adds its desired margin and adds it on top of the total costs to arrive at the final price to the customer. We have to consider two terms here which are often used interchangeably and cause confusion.

Mark-up is the amount the firm adds up to its total cost as a percentage. For example, if the total cost is Rs.100 and if the firm adds on a mark-up of 20% on its costs, the selling price will be Rs.120. The company makes a surplus of Rs.20.

On the other hand, margin is the money the company makes as a percentage of its selling price. In the above example, if we keep the same selling price of Rs.120 and the total costs remain at Rs.100, the margin works out to 20/120 = 16.67% only.

Thus, mark-up is based on cost to the company, while margin is on the selling price of the company.

- Competition-related pricing: Here, the company considers the prices of its leading competitors in the market in relation to the positioning and quality of their offerings compared to its own. Accordingly, it arrives at the pricing for the product. The company has to consider the bundle of benefits offered by competitors in relation to its own, including all benefits and promotions offered.

- Market-related or customer-related pricing: Most importantly, the company bases its pricing on the perception the consumers have about its product. As we had seen earlier, company looks at what value the customers place on its offering and what price they are willing to pay, considering the bundle of benefits and value offered to them.

It should be noted that companies cannot price their product based on any one of the above systems alone but have to take into consideration all factors mentioned under all these systems.

10.3 Cost-related pricing systems:

Under cost-related pricing, following are some of the alternative systems used by the companies to arrive at their selling price.

- Standard-cost pricing
- Marginal cost pricing
- Activity Based Costing (ABC) pricing

Activity Based Costing (ABC) system reflects cost per unit of product most accurately based on measuring all activities related to the product. It helps in identifying cost drivers, non-value adding activities and avoiding cross-subsidisation of one product by another. It is a potent strategic tool. However, most of the companies have not adopted this system since it is very complicated and collecting and maintaining required data on real time basis is very cumbersome.

10.4 Standard-cost pricing:

Under this system, products are called cost units and all direct costs that go into the product are allotted to that product unit. Cost centres where all activities take place- production cost centres and service cost centres- are created and all direct costs incurred by a particular cost centre are allotted to it. Indirect common costs that cannot be directly traced to the product are apportioned to the various cost centres based on some units of measure. For example, rent will be apportioned on the basis of floor area occupied by the cost centre, canteen expenses based on number of employees in that cost centre etc. These are then allotted to the product based on the usage of the cost centre. Thus, the product absorbs direct costs and indirect costs incurred at all cost centres to arrive at the total standard cost of the product. This consists of total direct costs like raw materials, manufacturing costs like machine-hour costs and other indirect overheads like sales, marketing, administration etc. The company then adds a suitable mark-up to arrive at its selling price.

This system works well as long as the market is not competitive. Also, there is cross-subsidisation of some products, with the result that true costs are not suitably reflected. In highly competitive markets, this system does not help since the company will not have the flexibility of changing prices of different products to meet market conditions.

10.5 Marginal-cost pricing:

i. From marketing point of view, especially on pricing decisions, marginal-cost pricing may be the more preferred approach. Here, all costs are classified based on their behaviour with volume of product produced as follows:

   - Fixed costs: They do not change with volume and remain constant until a given maximum level of production is reached and plant capacity is expanded. Examples of fixed costs include rentals, insurance, fixed salaries, periodic maintenance etc.

   - Variable costs: These change with volume directly. Variable costs include direct materials cost, direct labour cost, variable component of electricity bill etc. All costs that vary with volume come under variable costs.

   - On a per unit basis, we can see that as volumes go up, fixed costs per unit will come down and similarly as volumes drop, fixed costs per unit will go up. Variable costs per unit will remain the same even when the volumes vary.

ii. Contribution: We will now look at the concept of contribution which is defined as

Contribution per unit = Unit sales value or Unit selling price minus Unit variable costs

For example, if our selling price per unit is Rs. 100 and our total variable costs are Rs. 60 per unit,

Contribution per unit = Rs. 100 minus Rs. 60 = Rs. 40

This means to say that the extra money we make over and above variable costs goes towards contributing towards covering the fixed costs.

iii. Once we cover all the fixed costs, we will start making profits, as given below:

Total contribution = Sales volume in numbers x Contribution per unit

Profits = Total contribution – Total fixed costs

iv. Break-even volume: The point at which the company makes no profit or no loss is called the break-even point, expressed in the following equation:

Break-even volume (units) = Fixed costs (Rs.) divided by Contribution per unit (Rs.)

In our above example if the total fixed costs are Rs. 1,00,000 per year and contribution per unit is Rs. 40, then the break-even volume will be 1,00,000 divided by 40 = 2,500 units. Beyond this break-even volume, contribution per unit becomes profit per unit since all fixed costs are already covered.

v. Using marginal cost pricing method, we can see that after covering all fixed costs, we have the flexibility to reduce our selling price as long as we cover variable costs fully. In our example, after we reach the break-even sales volume of 2,500 units, if we have more capacity to produce, we can reduce our selling price to less than Rs.100 but greater than Rs. 60 which is our total variable cost.

This is especially useful when we have marketing opportunities at lower selling price, like export markets or any special pricing for bulk orders or specific customers that will result in additional volumes and profits.

10.6 Competition-related pricing:

Several alternative pricing strategies can be considered when we look at pricing in relation to competitors' prices.

- Price/market leadership: Companies who are leaders in their markets (in terms of volume/market share), have the flexibility of being price leaders as well. They set the prices and other competitors may have to follow their prices.

- Parallel or discount pricing: Here, depending on the reading of the market and competitive position of your product, you may price it parallel to the leader or your nearest competitor or at a discounted lower rate. "Follow the leader" is the strategy here.

- Penetration pricing: If you want to go deep down into the market and gain a bigger market share across all pricing points, you may resort to penetration pricing which will be the lowest at that pricing point in the market.

- Dumping: This is the last resort strategy when you are stuck with a lot of unsold inventory of your product.

10.7 Market/consumer related pricing:

Here again, companies have certain alternative approaches as follows:

- Perceived value pricing: The company will fix its selling price at a level where it feels that its customers think or perceive the company's product is worth that price. This is largely based on consumers' perception of the value your product is offering to them.

- Psychological pricing: This is a tactic where you make your price appear lower when in reality, it is only very marginally lower than a fixed psychological figure. The famous example is the tactic of Bata Shoes where they price their products at Rs. 1,999.90 to make it look much lower than Rs. 2,000.00!

- Promotional pricing: This is resorted to when either the product is at the introductory stage or has certain new features that are to be promoted.

- Skimming: Companies offering very high quality/value products but with limited capacity, resort to this strategy by which only select customers at the topmost layer of the market can afford to buy the product.

10.8 Other factors affecting pricing decisions:

It is to be emphasised that there is no one right way of pricing and that all pricing alternatives mentioned above like cost-based, competition-based and market/consumer -based pricing approaches need to be considered while fixing the price. In addition, following major factors also affect pricing decisions:

i.   Organisation's objectives: As we had seen in Booklet 2 on Organisations, companies can adopt one of the two broad generic strategies in running their business:

- Cost leadership: Lowest cost producer

- Differentiation leadership: Offering special features/ benefits to selected target segments, thus differentiating the company's product from competitors' offering.

From pricing strategy perspective, we can say that the company can adopt a low price/high volume or a high price/low volume strategy. In the first case, viz. low price/high volume strategy, the company looks for cornering a higher market share. In the latter case of high price/low volume strategy, the company may be looking in for a higher profit from limited volume or even market share.

As we had seen earlier, this depends on company's product positioning strategy, consumer perceptions, value delivered, offered/retained etc in relation to competition. This also depends on company's risk perceptions and preferences. While some may feel more comfortable or consider it less risky to sell higher volumes at lower prices, others may feel selling at higher prices and settling down for lower volumes may be less risky.

Market leaders are those who set the trend in both volumes and prices i.e., they dictate market prices and volumes.

ii. Product life cycle: This too is an important consideration. If your product is at the introductory stage with limited competition, you have the option of pricing it high or skimming the market. As you enter the growth stage, you may need to moderate your prices with promotional offers. At the maturity stage, it will become a price war and you need to concentrate on cutting costs and prices. If sales start declining, it will become more trade-oriented, with high discounts to trades/distribution channel partners.

iii.   External environment: Ultimately, like all business decisions, pricing also largely depends on developments in the external environment. As we saw, in the near environment, customers and competitors play a big role in your pricing decisions. In the far environment, economic, political and technological developments will dictate pricing strategy.

11.   Place/convenience:

The next "P" we will consider is Place or Convenience. This denotes the distribution channels we employ to reach our product from the place of manufacture to customers' residence. In a broader sense, it is a part of company's supply chain which encompasses the whole chain starting from the raw material manufacturer to the factory for conversion and ultimately to the consumers through distribution channels. In the current business environment dominated by faster and real time information and communication technologies and faster logistics and transportation facilities, raw materials and components can be sourced from any country in the world from suppliers who meet with your expectations of cost, quality, quantity and delivery schedule. Similarly, you are in a position to supply your finished products to consumers in every nook and corner of the world, provided they meet with their requirements and are competitive. Thus, Supply Chain Management (SCM) and Logistics Management (movement of goods) have become strategic tools. We will be covering these in greater detail in the booklet on "Managing Operations and the Supply Chain".

It is the primary responsibility of marketing to design, select and manage the company's distribution channels through which we reach our finished products to our customers. Efficiency, effectivity, cost, timely deliveries and agility- all these are important considerations in the design and selection of appropriate distribution channels.

11.1 Why have distribution:

Until recent years, the major function of marketing department was sales and distribution (S&D). Only with the emergence of consumer-centric marketing philosophy, other marketing functions like marketing research, advertising and sales promotion, marketing communication, product management etc began to get equal attention. It is no exaggeration to say that more than 75% of marketing department's time was being spent in managing sales and distribution functions.

The obvious answer to the question "why have distribution" is that customers can consume your products only if they are made available. Hence, the classic function of distribution is to ensure that "the right product is available at the right place at the right time in right quantities".

11.2 Major functions of distribution channels:

These can be summarised as follows:

- Availability: to make the product available as above through physical distribution
- Accessibility: to ensure that the customer has access to your products
- Render customer service: Many customer service activities take place at the point of delivery
- Facilitate communication: Similarly, consumers get a lot of information at the point of purchase apart from the opportunity to "touch and feel" the product before buying.

11.3 Normal distribution methods:

Only in the case of B2B products, that too where there are very few large business buyers, companies will be able to supply the product directly to the customers. In all other B2B products as well as in the case of bulk of B2C products or fast-moving consumer goods (FMCG), where company's present and potential customers are dispersed along the entire country, companies need to employ several layers of distribution channel members to reach and service their requirements. All these members form part of company's distribution channel. We will now look at some of the common methods of physical distribution.

i. As said earlier, in a few instances of B2B products, they are directly shipped from the company's factories to customers who are bulk buyers. In all other cases, companies create various stocking points or warehouses at vantage positions where the product is sold, through dealers or directly to smaller end-users in a particular area. This enable companies to take their products in bulk to the distribution centres or warehouses so that transportation costs can be kept low. From these stock points, smaller lots are transported to nearby end-users and dealer points.

ii. In the case of B2C or FMCG products, companies need to reach the mass market in every part of the country where their products are demanded. In such cases, depending on the nature of products and markets, different channel members come into play. The basic purpose of employing several layers of distribution is to make the products available as near to the customer as possible.

At the first level, FMCG companies normally have their warehouses or stock points, or employ services of companies who have warehousing or depot facilities in each region or state. From these points, goods are then transported to the next level of distributors- district-wise, area-wise or town-wise, depending on sales, market potential and costs involved. Different terms are used like distributors, authorised dealers, stockists etc with suitable distribution agreements. These distributors are entrusted with the primary task of distributing company's products to the next level, the retail shops. These retailers are the points of purchase for the consumers.

Thus, a typical distribution chain for FMCG products consists of warehouses/depots, distributors and retailers.

11.4 Other channels:

There are other channels like commission agents, wholesalers etc, who act as link between companies or distributors and retailers or end-users. Companies have their own showrooms to exhibit and sell entire range of their products, maintaining price parity with the distributors/ retailers to avoid price competition. There are a few multi-level chain marketers and companies who employ direct door-to door sales methods.

11.5 Modern trade:

To top it all, we are witnessing major changes in this classic chain. While the small retailers or corner shops still account for bulk of retail sales in our country, a new breed of huge chain departmental stores and other category sellers are making rapid strides. They operate through branches in several cities. These are called modern trade channels as opposite to traditional retail channels and this has completely transformed sales and distribution departments in companies.

11.6 On-line channels:

Finally, with the emergence of internet as a major force, we are all getting used to and do more and more of on-line buying. As I am in the process of writing this booklet, with the present all-pervasive pandemic situation, use of on-line buying is spreading fast even for low value consumable items. There are international giants like Amazon and large local players like Flipkart who are selling almost everything under the sun. They are market aggregators and many small manufactures use these platforms to reach the customers. Reputed large brands have also started on-line marketing in a big way, lest they become extinct. Convenience or ease of purchase has become as important as the brand image in the choice of even expensive products and brands.

11.7 Factors influencing selection of distribution channels:

From among this array of different methods, companies need to choose the most appropriate channel/s for their products based on the following factors:

- Markets & customers serviced and product sold: As we saw earlier, the distribution channels also called trade channels, are very closely linked to the markets they serve and products sold. Thus, distribution channels for FMCG products are different for B2B products. There are products like stationery items which need to be distributed only to specialist stationery outlets, bookshops and selected departmental stores whereas products like toffees and biscuits have to reach even the smallest of pan shops or corner stores.

- Organisational set-up: Generally, large organisations create their own selling and distribution departments to deal with trade channels so that they can have a high degree of control. Smaller organisations may have to depend on state-wise distributors and leave all distribution activities to them.

* Competition and external factors: Very often, the leader sets the norms for distribution channels in an industry and others follow. Availability of suitable distributors and their capabilities to offer required services are other factors to be considered in selecting suitable distribution channels.

11.8 Normal functions of distribution channel members:

Both the manufacturer or the parent company and customers have certain expectations from the distribution channel members. Normal services rendered by them include:

i. Ensuring greater width and depth of distribution: This ensures that the product is available to the customers at the nearest point, leading to greater reach and thereby higher market share for the company. Probably, this is the most important function of distribution. By width of distribution, we mean that the product should be made available as widely as possible in all areas in a given market. Depth of distribution indicates that in each area, all retail outlets are covered and product made available in all of them. These will lead to our product reaching the maximum number of potential customers and ensure higher market share.

ii. Holding stocks near the point of consumption: There is a lag between the time when the product is produced and when it reaches the customer. No company can produce the product just-in-time meaning, no company can produce and satisfy needs of customers dispersed widely, instantaneously. Also, companies have several products in several pack sizes etc in their range, each called a stock keeping unit or SKU. In order to ensure that the right product is available to the customer at the right time, there is a need to hold stocks at the point of purchase and this important function is carried out by the retailer/distributor.

iii. Giving financial shield: Financial strength, standing and reputation of the distributors are important considerations in the choice of distributors. Companies cannot be extending credit to individual customers/retailers because of financial risks involved. Invariably, distributors provide this service of extending credit facilities to retailers since they cover the markets regularly and have financial dealings with them. Company will be able to manage its cash flow by controlling its credit policy to distributors since they are fewer in numbers and company will be able to assess their financial strength on a continuous basis.

iv. Finally, retail shops are the last link in the distribution chain and the first point of direct contact with the end users. Hence, they are uniquely placed to communicate features of company's products to the customers and also give first-hand knowledge about customer preferences, their reaction to competitor activities and also general market conditions to the company. These are regularly collected by company's field staff when they visit them. Also, the retailers help company in maintaining customer relations, promotional activities and providing after sales service as required.

11.9 Channel members' compensation:

Of course, companies have to compensate distribution channel members for these services rendered by them. Normally, companies fix the recommended final selling price to the customers which is called the Maximum Retail Price (MRP) and this is printed/marked on the product. This is a legal requirement and ensures that while retailers are free to sell at lower prices, they cannot overcharge customers beyond the MRP. Based on this price to the consumers, companies work back, giving suitable margins to retailers, distributors etc to arrive at company's billing price. A typical price chain may be illustrated as follows:

Company's basic billing price on the distributors	:	Rs.100.00
Add sales tax (say) @10%	:	Rs.10.00
Add distributor margin @ 10% on company's basic Billing price	:	Rs. 10.00
Total=Distributors' billing price on retailers	:	Rs. 120.00
Add 15% margin to retailers on Rs.120.00	:	Rs. 18.00
Hence Maximum recommended retail price(MRP)	:	Rs. 138.00

These distributor and retailer margins depend on particular market practices invariably set by the market leader, company's relative market share and position, services expected of the channel members and their expectations on compensation etc. Other trade terms include credit facility extended by the company to the distributors or credit policy, transport allowances etc. These are covered under distributor contracts formally agreed upon by the company and distributor. As mentioned earlier, companies have their own set of criteria for selection and appointment of distributors like their financial strength, reputation in the market, storage and delivery facilities, sales manpower for covering the retail outlets etc. Distributor margins take into consideration costs of services rendered.

11.10 Channel conflict:

i.   From the above discussions, we can see that there is inherent scope for conflicts between the company and its distribution channel members. While the company will not be able to charge higher prices to consumers beyond its competitive position and consumers' perceptions and preferences, it has to part with a considerable part of its margin to the channel members like distributor and retailer margins. They will always be clamouring for greater margins which will only cut into company's profitability.

To a large extent, this will depend on the market position and market share of the company and also share of company's products sales in the distributors'/retailers' total sales. Market leaders will be able to squeeze them for lower margins since in many ways, major part of their sales and income depend on contribution from company's products. However, smaller players may have to part with higher margins since they need the channel members' support to place their products in retailers' shelves so that consumers can see them, pick them up and try them. In some product categories like pharmaceuticals, there are trade associations which dictate margins to be given by all manufacturing companies.

ii. Some of the ways in which channel conflicts can be minimised are:

•   Having clear agreement on goals to be achieved, services to be extended and commensurate compensation etc

•   Co-opting company salespersons to work with distributors' team to ensure required distribution and also training distributor salespersons in basic selling skills, product knowledge and company's sales policies

- Regular communication with channel members keeping them advised of company's plans, results etc
- Greater personal interactions at the appropriate levels

11.11 Exploring other methods:

As we saw earlier, with technological advancements in IT, Logistics etc, companies today are moving to reach the customers directly or with minimum number of intermediaries. The current raging Covid 19 pandemic has only exacerbated the problem and even middle- and lower-income group families have started buying their requirements online. Apart from metros and tier 1 cities, this trend is catching up in smaller towns also. Thus, role of traditional distribution channels is fast changing.

12. Promotion/Communication:

Very often, Promotion is thought to be the main subject of marketing. As we have just seen, all other elements of marketing mix are equally important since only when they are combined together based on the nature of the product or service and other considerations to satisfy a customer need, that we really land in a winning marketing strategy.

Sales Promotion and Communication can be considered as the two major subjects under this P - Promotion. We need to have a suitable communication/promotion mix to achieve the twin objectives of communicating with our customers and promoting our products and services to them. Normally, advertising is called the "pull strategy" since it is expected to pull or attract the customers to our offering. On the other hand, the "push strategy" consisting of various types of sales promotion is aimed at ensuring that our products become preferred choice at the time of purchase. We will deal with them separately in the following sections.

13. Advertising:

13.1 The communication process:

Advertising is part of communication process of the company. In the classical communication process model, there is a sender who codes the message he/she wants to convey in a particular manner, transmits it through suitable medium/media and the message is decoded by the receiver or audience of the message. Many times, due to shortcomings in various stages of this process and also due to external disturbances, the message may get distorted. The communication loop gets closed when there is feedback from the receiver/audience. In the case of advertising, it is reflected directly or indirectly by the changes in sales and market share as well as brand image.

In a lighter vein, in spite of sophisticated modern tools and techniques of communication and marketing research, the company does not really get to know which part of its advertising has worked and which one has not. This is humorously expressed by a former chairman of Unilever, one of the largest advertising spenders, as, "I know one half of my advertising is a waste, but I am not sure which half!"

13.2 How advertising works:

As we saw earlier, we use a framework called the AIUAPR model to see the purchase process of the customer.

A- Awareness: Getting to know about the product

I- Interest: Developing an interest to know more about the offering

U -Understanding: Understanding the features and benefits

A- Attitude: Developing a positive attitude towards the product

P- Purchase: Leading to purchasing

R- Repeat: Going for repeat purchase.

Thus, the various stages the customer goes through are self-explanatory. Advertising is supposed to work through these stages which is explained by another model called AIDA.

A- Awareness

I- Interest

D- Desire

A- Action

However, to what extent advertising alone can create this pull is debatable. Some believe that it does while others feel that it can only lead up to creating awareness and interest. Beyond that, it is customers' choice that dictates the purchase cycle.

13.3 Factors affecting advertising effectiveness:

It is normally expected that more and more money you spend on advertising, greater are the sales. However, beyond a certain level of advertising spend, sales will not grow and will remain constant or taper off due to various factors such as:

- Customer segment, product category, competitive situation and general economic conditions: General economic conditions impact the effect of advertising depending on the nature of the product and target customers. In good times, general public can afford to spend money on luxuries and their other unfulfilled wants and desires, whereas when the economy is down, they would like to conserve their money and postpone these purchases. However, the super-rich may not be affected by these downturns and super luxury products catering to them may still grow. We are witness to this tragedy of breakdown of general economic activities in almost all countries in the world in the wake of this pandemic and thousands of jobs have been lost affecting livelihoods of lakhs of people.

- Competitor advertising: It is like who spends more to attract customers, given quality and appeal are comparable in customer perception.

- Stage of growth of the sector and product life cycle: In a mature industry, the product would have moved away from growth stage and since most of the customers have more or less full knowledge of the company's product and competitive offerings, advertising will have limited impact. It may turn out to be more of promotion-based competition.

13.4 Two major aspects of advertising:

Basically, we can approach advertising strategy from two aspects - Message and Media. There is a saying that message is as good as the medium. Thus, both are intertwined and companies normally employ advertising agencies who recommend and on approval, implement the advertising plans.

13.5 The Message:

i.   There are copy writers who recommend the message or content of the advertising campaign based on the brief given by the company, indicating its product features and benefits, target audience, positioning strategy and its unique selling proposition (USP).

70

ii.   As we saw earlier, companies offer a package of physical, rational and emotional benefits to their target customers. They would like their customers to see them as offering the best value for money in their category.

These benefits are brought out in the advertising campaign through advertisements like press/print advertisements, TV spots, radio spots, outdoor media, social media etc. These are developed to send out the same message and reinforce the same brand image among target customers to make the necessary impact on them. This is creative part of advertising.

iii.   Normally, a press ad consists of a headline, a body copy, a visual and a sign-off or tagline - all taken together, reinforcing the positioning message in the minds of the target customer.

A TV spot is normally woven around a story depicting a potential customer with a need or want and the advantages of using the company's offering in fulfilling that need or want. Celebrities are also widely used to endorse the product.

Radio spot is often a jingle to create immediate awareness and recognition of the brand by frequent association.

A spot in social media may be a combination of all these elements.

There are many creative ways in which the creative personnel in the advertising agencies develop the message/theme in the advertisements. They base it on the profile of target audience, product category, the positioning strategy of the company and the media used. They try to maximise the impact of their advertisements by developing unique and attractive story and weave them around it. This is more so because of ever-increasing clutter and noise levels in all media and resultant ever-shrinking attention span of customers. Advertising Associations offer several awards for outstanding advertisements, which are considered prestigious and help in improving client base and revenue for these agencies.

13.6 The Media:

In today's customer-driven world, companies use every opportunity to catch the eyes/attention of the customer and there is an explosion of media available to get the message across to the customer.

Main among them are:

i.   Press: This is the print medium and you have dailies, weeklies, bi-weeklies, monthlies etc in English and vernacular languages, each having its own rates based on its readership, readers' profile, space or size for the ad and frequency of releases.

ii. TV/cinema/mobile phones and all other visual/video media: Apart from mind-boggling number of TV channels, all modern digital platforms like internet, social media etc form the range of media while cinema and radio continue to be popular. Costs of these are dictated by the time of the slot, duration and frequency required.

iii. There are also other traditional media like outdoor hoardings, mobile vans and point-of-sale media like banners, posters, name boards, in-shop displays etc.

iv. Direct mailers both in postal and electronic media and telemarketing etc are also extensively used. Innovative use of media often leads to high effectivity at low costs.

13.7 Advertising strategy and budget:

As we saw earlier, the overall company strategy and marketing strategy in terms of marketing objectives, targeting and positioning strategies and other marketing mix elements decide the advertising strategy.

Even with the best of measures, it is difficult to exactly determine the effectiveness and impact of advertising. Advertising agencies use sophisticated models to decide on the media mix. These models give the optimum mix primarily based on your target audience, how many of them you want to reach with your advertising campaign (reach), the number of opportunities for them to see your ad (OTS), cost of each of the chosen media etc. Companies also decide whether the advertisements should be released in concentrated bursts or spent over an extended period called burst vs. drip strategy. Apart from all these, two main factors that dictate the advertising budget are: competitive advertising spend and how much the company itself can afford to spend on its advertising and communication efforts.

13.8 Sales promotions:

Just like advertising media, there are myriad sales promotional measures that are available to companies to promote their products to create the "push" effect. We can broadly classify them into three groups: those aimed at customers, at the trade and at company's own sales force.

i. Consumer promotions may be money based like price-offs, goods or product based like toothbrush with tooth paste and one free for 12 etc or service based like add-on guarantees, free admission to events like cinema shows, musical concerts etc.

ii.   Trade promotions are given both to distributors and retailers. They range from volume discounts, target-based incentives, extended credit, free gifts, free trips to tourist places, overseas locations etc. Other promotions include awards like "Best dealer" membership to company's Chairman's club" etc.

iii. For the sales force, company's offer target-based bonuses, free gifts, free trips and awards like "Best salesperson" at annual sales conferences etc.

All these should enthuse consumers, trade channel members and sales personnel to buy/stock/sell more of company's products and remain committed to them.

iv.   Sales promotional schemes offer several advantages:

   •   They can be directed at the exact target audience.

   •   They can be time bound unlike price reductions.

   •   Will result in short-term increase in sales.

V.   Disadvantages:

   •   They are often short lived.

   •   If they are continued on a long-term basis, the beneficiaries tend to discount them and they may not produce desired results.

   •   They may also damage company's brand image as "the one that can be sold only with discounts and offers".

13.9 The other 3 Ps relating to Marketing of Services:

Since Services Marketing needs a slightly different approach, 3 more Ps were added to the marketing mix- People, Process and Physical evidence. Since Services are sold or rendered and consumed or used at the same time, these become important.

- People rendering the service
- The entire Process of finding out consumer requirements, attending to them, executing, raising bills and collecting payments
- The ambience of the service outlet like the retail shops etc which reflect on the quality serving as Physical evidence

All these add to the experience of the consumer which decides his/her revisit/repurchase as well as loyalty and hence form an important part of your marketing strategy.

13.10 Public Relations (PR):

Another strategy for building up and enhancing the company's image as well as that of its products and services is through public relations. Here, the company communicates not only with its customers and trade channel members but also with public at large. This is done through media advertising on general topics, media interviews, participating in exhibitions, seminars etc. In large organisations, there is often a separate corporate PR department concentrating exclusively on this strategy.

14. Personal selling:

i. From the time the marketing concept moved from seller orientation to buyer orientation, personal selling has been a major element of marketing strategy. In the recent years, with the growth of Information and Communication technologies and real time data-driven world, the nature of personal selling has changed considerably. It still remains a major tool in the marketer's kit. However, with continuing onslaught of Covid 19 pandemic which has totally disrupted the way customers buy and products are sold, it is anybody's guess whether personal selling will retain its pre-eminent position.

ii.   In initial periods, companies resorted to very aggressive selling techniques and recruited salespersons with similar attitude and behaviour. This led to a bad reputation for sales profession and salespersons were considered as "predators" bouncing on unsuspecting and gullible customers and dumping on them all unwanted stuff. This image persists, though not to the same extent. In fact, selling could be a very exciting and satisfying career for those who are outgoing and like meeting people and possess necessary aptitude and skills. Developing and maintaining long lasting relationships and thorough product knowledge are the cornerstones for a successful sales career.

We can say that everyone in the organisation plays a part in this relationship building, though for the customer, the salesperson is the first point of contact with the organisation.

iii.   It is said that there are two types of salespersons classified as "Hunters" and "Farmers". Hunters are persuasive and are good at delivering immediate results whereas farmers are good at developing relationships and exhibit empathy and consistency, often acting as problem solvers for the customers in the long run.

In B2B markets, relationships matter though sound product knowledge, maintaining regular face-to-face contacts, developing trust and acting as a problem solver or advisor are primary requisites. On the other hand, in B2C markets, sales representatives often meet up with distributors and normally do not come in contact with end-user. Here, planning routes and making calls, frequent and scheduled market coverage, communicating about company's product features and policies effectively to trade members and closing sales are required. They need to have strong goal/target orientation.

iv. Many tasks are performed by salespersons. Forecasting, planning, making presentations and communicating, closing sales, collecting outstanding payments, new account prospecting, projecting the right image of the company and its products among customers and trade through proper behaviour- these are some of the major tasks performed by them.

15. Marketing organisation:

From the above discussions, we can see that marketing departments have to perform several functions and they are designed accordingly depending on organisation's requirements, nature of customers and markets served, product/services sold etc. They also depend on the size of the organisation, objectives, orientation and philosophy of owners/senior managers. In any case, companies would do well to keep in mind the marketing concept, viz, the primacy of the customer in their businesses. The major functions can be grouped into:

i. Product Management: This plays an important role in co-ordinating all activities relating to a particular product from design stage to final sales. In FMCG companies the primary role is finalising and implementing company's communication strategy in terms of advertising, sales promotion etc. In B2B markets, understanding customer requirements, communicating product's features and capabilities, help customer in problem solving, relationship building etc are the major functions.

ii. Sales and Distribution Management: This is the backbone of marketing department especially in FMCG companies. Sales planning, managing sales force, managing distribution channel members etc are the primary functions with direct responsibility for achieving sales targets and budgets.

iii. Marketing Services Management: All services relating to customers and trade etc- billing, collection of outstanding payments, complaint handling- these are handled here with active support and co-ordination with salespeople.

iv. Marketing Research and Marketing Data Management: In large companies, planning for research, conducting and evaluating research findings and managing marketing data and advising senior managers on these are the tasks performed here.

16. Marketing metrics:

As we say, only what gets measured, gets done. Companies use different measures to evaluate their marketing performance and some of the common metrics used are:

i. Company's profits: Ultimately, all marketing efforts should lead to achievement of profit objectives of the company.

ii. Total sales: Meeting sales targets as per plan gets measured.

iii. Market share: Companies can grow only when they maintain their marketing share in a mature market or grow faster than industry in a growing market.

iv. Sales achieved per sales staff: This is to measure whether sales and support activities produce effective results for the manpower employed.

v. Effectiveness of advertising and communication: Though this may be difficult to measure directly, this is related to total sales, awareness levels of company's products and brands among consumers, brand image, brand perception etc.

vi. Number of new products launched, number of new customers acquired, their share of total sales etc: These are measured to understand whether the company is positioning itself for the future consisting of emerging technologies and products, customer groups etc.

17. Integrative marketing processes:

We have covered the major concepts of segmentation, targeting, positioning, understanding customer through marketing research, marketing mix etc in the preceding sections. These form the basis on which marketing strategies of companies are developed and implemented.

However, the business world is becoming more and more complex because of major changes that are causing constant turbulence and we need to look at new ways of doing things to meet these challenges.

i.   External environment is constantly churning and we cannot predict future with any certainty.

ii. Globalisation and liberalisation have changed the nature of markets and competition.

iii. Changing demographics and cross-country influences have changed the ways people live and buy things.

iv. Constantly evolving new technologies that are making yesterday's best practices obsolete.

17.1 Integrative processes:

While the marketing framework which we had seen so far is still robust, we need to look at following integrative marketing processes that are becoming the cornerstones of a company's marketing success while it meets the challenges of change. It is especially becoming critical in these Covid 19 pandemic times.

i.   Managing relationships

ii. Building and managing brand equity

iii. Integrating all marketing communication

17.2 Managing relationships:

More than ever, managing relationships has become critical since only through relationships, you can hope to maintain your customer base in these challenging times. Relationships at personal level, company/corporate level as well as brand level are all important in this endeavour. Some of the basic considerations in managing relationships are:

i.   Acquiring new customers is much more expensive than maintaining existing customer base intact. You can work out the lifetime value of a customer from your present sales to the customer, growth in sales over time, relative share of your sales to this customer in your total sales, your share of their purchase in their total purchases, customer's technological capabilities and your association in this regard etc.

ii. You have to move your relationship up the ladder from a prospect and customer to advocate and partner.

iii. Key customers need to be identified based on factors given in point (i) and nurtured

iv. Loyal customers will stay with you and will even forgive your occasional mistakes.

v.   You need to find the gaps in your service levels and communications with the customer and take effective steps to plug them.

vi. It is essential that you develop and implement a data-based "Customer Relationship Management" (CRM) system which helps in acquiring, servicing and retaining your customers that enables you to cross-selling and up-selling of your products and services so that you grow with the customers.

17.3 Building brand and brand equity:

Prof. Kevin Lane Keller has outlined the strategic brand building process in his book "Strategic Brand Management", given under primary reference books.

i. We can summarise the brand building process as follows:
- Create basic anchor values that define your brand
- Find out customer perceptions and preferences through sound marketing research methods
- Decide on your customer value proposition consisting of tangible and intangible benefits
- Position your product in the minds of your target customer by effective positioning strategy
- Develop and implement your promotional strategy consisting of advertising and sales promotions

ii. Creating customer-based brand equity (CBBE) alone will ensure loyal customers for your brand. This can be done by providing the right kind of experience to the customers through desired thoughts, feelings and perceptions

iii. Brand equity consists of higher degree of brand awareness and strong, favourable brand image.

iv. You can create a strong brand awareness through ensuring a high degree of brand recall and brand recognition by customers through your communication as well as product and packaging design.

v. Your brand should be at the top of your target customers' mind in their awareness, consideration and choice.

vi. In creating unique brand image, the challenge is to establish what product category your brand belongs to and in what ways it is different from other brands in the market. The former is by communicating points of parity with the category and the latter is through your unique selling proposition (USP) highlighting the points of difference.

vii. Major sources through which you can create strong brand image are:

- Product/service characteristics
- Providing right kind of direct experience to your target customers
- Word-of-mouth support by creating required "buzz"
- By judicious blend of your marketing mix elements
- Communication through peer/user groups
- Endorsements from influencers consisting of experts, channel members etc

viii. You can create strong brand image through establishing strong association by linking your product's features, attributes and benefits (FAB) to customers' rational and emotional needs.

ix. Thus, your complete brand building strategy should consist of creating necessary awareness, image and relationship in the minds of the customer:

You need to build in rational, emotional and other psychological benefits so that customer sees your brand as the most appropriate one for him/her. This is the objective of the customer-based brand building process.

17.4 Integrating marketing Communication:

In the present-day world where there are so many forces competing to gain customer's attention, it is imperative that you project the same image of your product/brand in all ways your customer comes in contact with it. These are called customer "touch points", starting with the product itself. Some of the primary touch points are:

- Product design (look, feel and performance)
- Pricing
- Distribution
- Advertising and other communication messages
- Sales promotions
- People, Process and Physical evidence in the case of services
- Customer service- pre and post sales
- Continuous relationship-building activities

Customer's perception of your product and brand is created, sustained and reinforced at each one of these touch points. Companies should strive to project consistent and favourable image at all these points. This is the essence of integrating all the communication efforts.

17.5 Summing up:

i. I have highlighted these three key marketing processes here primarily because in these turbulent times, we can hope to maintain our position in the market only through establishing, maintaining and building up further our relationship with the customers in terms of people, products and brands. Hence Customer relationship

Management (CRM), building brands and brand equity and implementing integrated communication efforts- these take the central stage in our marketing strategy to ensure that our customers stay with us through thick and thin.

ii. However, even as I am giving finishing touches to this section, Covid 19 virus continues to play havoc with our lives. In spite of temporary abatement and commencement of vaccination on a mass scale in our country and all over the world, the pandemic has totally disrupted the way we live, learn and do things. With economy taking a battering and newer developments in communication technologies everyday, all our actions based on conventional and non-conventional wisdom are undergoing profound changes. On one hand, many people will scale down their needs and settle for value brands offering basic functional benefits rather than those which offer high value in terms of emotional and self-expressive benefits. On the other hand, there is a segment consisting of rich and super-rich people who are least affected by these developments and continue to live as before. To what extent our marketing efforts will sustain us through the pandemic is anybody's guess.

18. Developing marketing strategies:

18.1 Basis for marketing strategies:

What we have seen so far as listed below, form the basis for developing our marketing strategies:

- Customer orientation
- Analysing the external marketing environment consisting of the wider business environment and competition

- Understanding customer needs and wants based on continuous marketing research findings
- Finalising marketing objectives based on above analysis of environment, competition and customers and in line with company's overall objectives and strategies
- Segmentation, targeting and positioning strategies
- Formulating and managing elements of marketing mix-product, price, place and promotion
- Giving focus to the three major processes of customer relationship management, building brands and brand equity and integrating communication

Based on these, companies normally develop a basic formal document called the Marketing Plan which outlines all the above factors leading to their comprehensive marketing strategies. The marketing plan serves as the reference document for all marketing actions and results achieved are monitored against the objectives outlined in the marketing plan.

18.2 Major tools and techniques:

There are several tools and techniques which are used in formulating these marketing strategies and some of the major tools are listed below:

i. Value chain: This model is used to analyse our organisation by breaking it down into sequential parts in terms of primary and secondary activities. We then compare each activity to see where we stand with respect to competition, benchmark with best practices followed by market leaders in our own industry and other industries so that we can bring in necessary improvements to bring down and control our costs and add value. This is helpful in developing competitive advantage.

ii. SWOT analysis: We use SWOT analysis - strengths, weaknesses, opportunities and threats –to assess our competitive position that should help us in minimising/ eliminating our weaknesses, building our strengths, preparing to meet threats and exploring new opportunities.

iii. Generic strategies: Broadly, companies can adopt any one of the following strategies for business and our marketing strategy to be developed to fall in line. The two broad generic strategies are: cost leadership or differentiation for competitive advantage.

iv. Product/Market development: We have seen that products follow a life cycle with introduction, growth, maturity and decline stages and profits from them also follow a similar pattern. In order to achieve our growth objectives in terms of profits, sales and market share, we need to decide where to put our promotional money and keep developing new products. There are generally four paths to achieve this:

• Greater market penetration – existing products, existing markets

• Product development – new products, existing markets

• Market development – existing products, new markets

• Diversification – new products, new markets

These are developed by a 2x2 matrix, called Ansoff matrix, named after Russian mathematician. However, defining what exactly you mean by products and markets is a challenging task and is subject to different interpretations. Also, this does not consider competitive scenario.

v. Product portfolio matrix: This is called BCG matrix after the consulting firm, Boston Consulting Group, who had developed this framework. Potential market growth for the product category and your product's market share in relation to the market leader are used in the matrix to plot the products. Company's products falling in the four sections of the graph are designated with the following labels:

- Dog: Here, both potential market growth and your relative share are low for this product and as such, this product should be discarded.

- Cash cows: These are products where the potential market growth is low, but your relative share is high. Hence you should maximise your profit from them and use the profits generated for developing new products.

- Question marks: These are new products being developed by you. Here, both market growth potential and your relative share are low in an emerging situation. You have to nurture them and convert them to Stars.

- Stars: In these products, both market growth potential and your relative market share are high. You continue to support them till the market reaches saturation when they will become cash cows.

To summarise, the logic is as follows:

- Kill dogs
- Milk cash cows
- Develop question marks
- Sustain stars

Thus, at any given point of time, you will have balancing products in your portfolio.

18.3 Marketing strategies and tactics:

In general, we can say that all short-term decisions to combat competition and meet your sales targets will fall under tactical measures. Examples are: short-term sales promotions, temporary addition to sales force for extra coverage of the market etc. Strategic decisions are often holistic and long-term oriented, setting the direction for all marketing activities. However, in these turbulent and uncertain times, this approach needs to be modified to the extent that strategy has to be continuously monitored and reviewed and specific aspects need to be modified based on emerging market situations. We can appropriately call it as dynamic approach to strategy. However, the short-term tactical moves and adjustments should be aligned to long term strategic objectives which are based on company's vision, mission and values.

If the company misses achieving its objectives of profit growth, sales growth, market share etc continuously, the whole set of strategic assumptions and approaches should be reviewed and revamped comprehensively in line with customers' needs and perceptions, and emerging technologies. This is the top and bottom line of marketing strategy- aligning your strategy to present and emerging customer needs.

19.   Taking Marketing "Beyond Marketing:

I am of the view that enlarging the scope of marketing or taking marketing beyond marketing is tantamount to enlarging the scope of the company's/corporate's business itself. I firmly believe that Marketing should go beyond its present boundaries for the organisation to play a larger role in shaping the future of societies. I am afraid the famous words of Dr. Milton Friedman, winner of Nobel Prize for Economic Sciences in 1976 that "the business of business is business" which dominated much of business philosophy in the late 20th century, is not relevant anymore.

As the window of the organisation to the outside world and as the representative of customers' and society's voice in the organisation, there is a need to enlarge the scope of marketing to enable companies to play a greater role in solving major challenges facing societies today. I list below some of the major areas where Marketing can play a leading role in shaping the corporate's overall efforts in this direction:

- Aiming for a purpose higher than just making profits and maximising return and adding on to the shareholders' wealth

- Limiting the evils of "consumerism", excessive materialism, conspicuous consumption and waste

- Communicating and assisting in instilling lasting values and greater purpose than consumption among consumers

- Participating actively in collaborative initiatives in tackling society's problems with other organisations

More than ever, with the devastating effects of Covid 19 pandemic on humanity, there is a need to initiate a paradigm shift in our whole approach to business and marketing.

Primary reference books

1. Study Materials for B-800: Foundations of Senior Management By the Open University Business School, UK

2. Marketing 3.0: From Products to Customers to the Human Spirit (2010) By Philip Kotler, Hermawan and Iwan Setiawan

3. Marketing Management: A South Asian Perspective (13th Edition - 2009)) By Philip Kotler, Kevin Lane Keller, Abraham Koshy and Mithileshwar Jha

4. Strategic Brand Management: Building, Measuring and Managing Brand Equity (2nd Edition - 2007) By Kevin Lane Keller

5. Mastering Management 2.0: Your Single-Source Guide to Becoming a Master of Management By Financial Times: Edited by James Pickford (2004)

6. Organisational behaviour (11th Edition - 2006) By Stephen P. Robbins and Seema Sanghi

7. Key management ratios: The 100+ ratios every manager needs to know (Fourth edition - 2008) By Ciaran Walsh

8. Contemporary Strategy Analysis (Third Edition - 1998) By Robert M. Grant.

Afterword

I started writing the booklet on Basics of Business Management and subsequent booklets covering each block by end of 2019. So far, I have completed four booklets and two more remain. The Covid 19 pandemic hit the world right through this period of end 2019, whole of 2020, 2021 and third and fourth waves are on us right now since January 2022. It has shaken the very basics of our lives to a great extent. As a consequence, whatever is written here has to be seen in this changed context. While all the basic and classic ideas presented here are equally applicable in the present circumstances, we need to modify the ways in which we apply them in the present context.

For example, work from home and online meetings have become the new norms in inter and intra office meetings involving white collar jobs. However, one can see a yearning as well as reluctance to get back to normalcy as soon as possible with abatement of the pandemic. Similarly, the phenomenal growth of online shopping has changed the ways in which products are promoted, stored, bought and delivered. These have given way to new business opportunities and have also led to the demise of many established ones. Integrated global supply chains are fraying at their ends to meet the supplies and demands from various parts of the world.

Driving all these is the relentless growth of the digital technologies. While this has brought in several advantages, it has also created many challenges. Navigating business in the digital world is the basic challenge faced by all companies and their managers.

With greater penetration of social media, people in all countries have become more aware of developments all over the world. As seen earlier, this has revolutionised the way people see and buy products and services. Brand loyalty based purely on premium image by multinational corporations (MNCs) is taking a beating with the emergence of "value for money" shift in consumer's minds. While more avenues for finance are available, pressures to control costs and offer robust profits to shareholders are proving to be great challenges in managing the finances of organisations.

Further, this has also brought in greater awareness among people on growing inequalities. It is an established fact that the rich, especially the very rich, have grown disproportionately rich and the poor, the bottom of the pyramid, have become poorer. Women empowerment as well as emerging groups like LGBT (lesbian, gay, bisexual and transgender) all need recognition and expect acceptance and opportunities available to others. Organisations cannot just stop at paying lip service to the concept of 'equal opportunity employer' but need to implement the same in letter and spirit.

In the current global political scenario, the so-called "superpowers" are flexing their muscles and are becoming more and more protective of their industries and territories. Emerging nations, having suffered suppression by them are also jostling for niche space more vigorously. A unipolar world that existed with the demise of Soviet Union is once again witnessing great rivalries between the two economic superpowers of USA and China. Both of them and Russia are vying to be the leader in the global context with financial, trade and military might and unbridled ambition for expanding their territories and spheres of influence. These conflicts have created great tension and flareup among them and other nations which have aligned with them all over the world. At the same time, threat of nuclear warfare by any indiscriminate ruler in any one of these countries hangs heavily in the air and the United Nations has been reduced to a mute spectator. These have led to authoritarian leaders in many countries and democratic values and freedom of thought and expression have been curtailed.

How true this has played out is being seen by the unexpected invasion of Ukraine by Russia, started in February 2022. This war has been dragging on till today causing much human misery and disturbing the whole world with prospects of massive hunger caused by sudden breakdown of supply chains. The comity of nations is getting fractured, and the threat of nuclear warfare appears real. As far as business and management fields are concerned, companies have gone back to drawing boards to rewrite their supply chain configurations even as they have just started implementing new supply chain strategies as a fallout of Covid 19. Once again, inequalities are rising and while new millionaires are springing up fast, millions of people are staring at abject poverty.

With the devastating blow delivered by Covid 19, governments have once again become the major economic engines in most of these nations. Giant technological corporations that dominate the digital world are fighting fiercely to protect their turfs as well as make inroads into others' domains. In the process, they are dictating the ways we, the people, live since our modern lives depend on them. Governments are finding it more and more difficult to rein them in due to their financial and market powers.

Most of the world is facing the reality of environmental degradation and the growing green movement to protect the globe for the present and future generations is gathering force.

All these have naturally affected all organisations' priorities, objectives, strategies etc.

Summing up, we can say that "business as usual" or old ways of doing things will not work anymore. New, innovative ways need to be found to meet these challenges constantly in this ever-changing scenario. However, I would like to emphasise that these basic, classic concepts and ideas still hold good, and we need to modify the ways we practise them. The basic purpose of these booklets is to expose the readers to all these classic concepts that have stood the test of time in a simple and concise manner so that they can start thinking and working out how to put them in practice in the current context.

A.S. Srinivasan   **October, 2022**

A.S. Srinivasan

A.S. Srinivasan holds a bachelor's degree in Mechanical Engineering (from the University of Madras), a Post Graduate Diploma in Plastics Engineering (D.I.I.T. from the Indian Institute of Technology, Bombay) and a Master's degree in Business Management (M.B.M. from the Asian Institute of Management, Manila, Philippines). He has participated in the Global Program for Management Development of the University of Michigan Business School.

Srinivasan has over 25 years of experience in industry and 15 years of experience in academics and consulting. His industry experience is primarily in the areas of Marketing and General Management in companies like TI Cycles, Aurofood, Pierce Leslie and Cutfast.

His last assignment was with Chennai Business School, a start up business school in Chennai, for over two years. As the first Dean of the school, he developed and implemented the curriculum for the post graduate program in management for the first batch. Prior to that, he was working with Institute for Financial Management and Research (IFMR), Chennai, for 8 years looking after the partnership with the Open University Business School (OUBS), UK in offering their Executive MBA in India. Apart from handling courses in the PGDM program of IFMR, he was actively involved in offering Management Development Programs (MDPs) to corporates and in consultancy assignments.

His current interests are in the areas of Management, Business, Economics etc. where he would like to keep himself updated with recent developments. He has taken to publishing blogs on these subjects for private circulation.

A.S. Srinivasan
A1/3/4, "Srinivas", Third Main Road,
Besant Nagar, Chennai 600 090
Mobile: 91 98414 01721
Email: sansrini@gmail.com

Printed in Great Britain
by Amazon

42530023R00056